One Red Rooster

Kathleen Sullivan Carroll

Illustrated by Suzette Barbier

Houghton Mifflin Company Boston 1992

For Sean Cody —K.S.C.

For my husband, Cyrus, and my son, Andrew —S.B.

Library of Congress Cataloging-in-Publication Data

Carroll, Kathleen Sullivan.
One red rooster / Kathleen Sullivan Carroll ; illustrated by Suzette Barbier.
p. cm.
Summary: Introduces the numbers one through ten in rhymed text and illustrations of a variety of rather noisy farm animals.
ISBN 0-395-60195-9
[1. Stories in rhyme. 2. Counting. 3. Domestic animals—Fiction. 4. Animal sounds—Fiction.] I. Barbier, Suzette. ill. II. Title.
PZ8.3.C2340n 1992 91-17271
CIP
[E]—dc20 AC

Printed in the United States of America

HOR 10 9 8 7 6 5 4 3 2 1

One Red Rooster

1 One red rooster went cock-a-doodle-doo

2 Two black cows

went moo moo moo

3 Three blue birds

went tweet tweet tweet

4 Four white sheep

went bleat bleat bleat

5 Five orange cats

went meow meow meow

6 Six gold dogs

went bow wow wow

7 Seven brown horses

went neigh neigh neigh

8 Eight gray donkeys

went bray bray bray

9 Nine yellow chicks

went peep peep peep

10 And ten pink pigs

fell fast asleep

1 2 3 4 5 6 7 8 9 10